IRREPLACEABLE

A LIFE OF A YOUNG WOMAN FIGHTING FOR HER FREEDOM.

REAPER

ISBN 979-888569588-6

This book is dedicated to one of the most important people in my life, who is the best at bringing me back to my senses and in whom I have complete faith. If you are that person, you will certainly be aware of it.

Contents

Preface

The names of the characters in this book were changed to remain anonymous because it contains many heart-breaking incidents and it was about a girl who faced many hardships in her life but still managed to face them, and she was utterly depressed at one point in her life but she refused to give up and fought back.

Prologue

It isn't a fairytale to begin with "Once upon a time, ..."
. This is based on a true tale about a girl who encountered
numerous challenges in her life but overcame them all with
a grin on her face.

Since this isn't a biography, let's pretend that it is a
fairytale without any fairies.

Let us begin with her childhood.

Everyone grows up in diverse circumstances, with
varied ambitions and goals, and their dreams differ from
one another. Not everyone is born with a silver spoon; they
must work really hard to achieve their goals and ambitions.

Some are nurtured in a depressed, chaotic, or strict
environment, while others are nurtured in a happy, trouble-
free environment.

Everyone does not have free will at birth; some are
influenced by their parents, while others are influenced
by their relatives, and they are largely influenced by the
opinions of others; yet, everyone want to live without
limitations and with their freedom in their hands.

Similarly, the protagonist of our novel is brought up in
a tight setting that has elements of sorrow, chaos, and joy.
She has always had huge dreams and wishes to do many
things on her own, without the assistance of others. She
may have been reared in a rigid household, but she has
always been a kind-hearted, honest, helpful, open-minded,
and optimistic person who is always willing to help anyone
in need.

Well to be anonymous let's name our protagonist as
Emma.

CHAPTER ONE

Emma had a difficult infancy; She had a small section of her intestine spilling from her body after her birth, and surgeons were able to perform the necessary surgery and rescue her.

Her father's workplace is elsewhere than where she grew up, and her mother has done an outstanding job raising both of her children. On weekends, her father would pay them a visit, and he would always take her for a haircut. So she's had her hair cut short for a time now, and it suits her perfectly. She missed her father a lot, but she never told anyone about it; instead, she kept it to herself. She felt lonely at those times because she didn't get to spend time with all of her family members.

Emma adores her grandma since she is always there for her and never fails to encourage her in each and everything. Her grandma is the person she loves the most.

She attended a girls' school for her education. She is a sensitive individual who is incapable of blaming others even if they have committed a mistake. She can't debate with anyone, and she gets upset easily.

She used to spend the majority of her time daydreaming about unattainable goals. She wasn't doing well in school at first, so her parents enrolled her in private tutoring, where she excelled in mathematics and developed a strong interest in the subject. Since then, she has continued to learn everything from the basics to the most advanced concepts, never abandoning any concept because she loves and enjoys doing math.

Basically she became an expert in the mathematics when compared with her friends and for the exam results she just checks whether she did good in math's and ignores all the remaining subjects.

She isn't outgoing because her parents used to be strict about her schedule, and she also doesn't have much time to do things because she spends the most of her time in tuitions and school. When she gets home after tuition, she does her homework and then goes straight to bed since she is exhausted.

Emma tries to appreciate the little things in her life and does not want to miss any good moments. She wants each and every moment in her life to be memorable.

She enjoys singing and dancing, and as a hobby, she has taken traditional dance lessons. She even performed the dance she had learnt, but she stopped doing it when she was in eighth grade. She still does it occasionally at home when her mother asks her to do so.

Her attitude shifted once she completed 10th grade, and she became a completely different person with short-tempered, arrogant, and confrontational behavior. She had a crush on a boy in her college who she used to stalk every day. She started liking him, but there was a lot of competition for him, which landed her into trouble. Some of her college classmates used to tease her about his crush, and she once became enraged and retaliated, which was an intimidating moment in her life up to that point.

She used to have a close group of friends in college, and it was one of the most rewarding experiences she has ever had. Emma bunked lot of classes with her pals, which are part of her life's highlights. In her intermediate, she had the most fun. She had a lot of nice friends in college, and during exams, they all used to cheat together, which meant that their marks were all in the same range.

Emma enjoys her college life because she was a tomboy in college, more vocal, and she teases their pals, as well as the other way around. She has most of the memorable memories from her college.

Her crush used to approach her, but she never had the courage to tell him she was interested in him, despite the fact that she had a secret crush on him, which isn't really a secret because everyone on campus knows about it except for him. Even if he was aware, he would not confront her because he had other plans for someone he liked.

On a nice day in her college, as she was passing by, one guy made fun of her about his crush, and she was angered by it, so she argued with him and warned him not to mess with her again, and everyone was surprised to see her in rage and no one dared to interrupt her.

Emma and her crush used to talk to one other and were good friends, but she was still obsessed with him. However, he was rude and arrogant, and Emma gradually developed a dislike for him because he always tried to take away her freedom. She does not get to pick what she does. As a result, she sought to avoid him. It was difficult for her at first, but she continued and managed to get herself out of that mess.

Her crush was in a different relationship at the time, and it was with one of her classmates. She used to tell her crush lies about Emma and others, which made him dislike Emma, but she was fine with it.

When it came to her college, she was more extroverted than she was at school because her parents gave her the freedom to do whatever she wanted as long as it didn't interfere with her academics.

Emma spent much of her time in college having fun, which resulted in her receiving poor results in her final examinations. She worked hard to prepare for the improvement exams, but her luck ran out.

She had a best friend since she was in second grade, and they used to have a lot of fun together and spend most of their time together during school. However, because they were not in the same college, Emma missed her a lot, so after completing the +2, they decided to join in the same college, and it happened exactly as they wished. They both joined in the same field for their bachelor's degrees.

CHAPTER TWO

Emma made some acquaintances after starting university and was loving everything that was going on around her, such as skipping lectures and chatting with pals.

After a few days, she made some friends Peter, Steve and they began supporting each other in college with their academics, and their bond grew slowly to the point where they began to have fun talking to each other and they used to spend quite a bit of time together, and they formed their own social media groups and began conference calls each day to discuss whatever they had done in college.

Everything was OK until rumors began to circulate that she was dating Peter, which was untrue, but they became stronger with each passing day and began to spread around the college without her knowledge. Everyone began to treat her differently, and she never questioned anyone about it.

After a few days, rumors began to surface that she was dating both of them at the same time and that she was using them for her own objectives. She was unaware of this because no one had informed her of it. She made another buddy alongside the two of them, and his name is Harry he doesn't get along with Peter and Steve. They aren't best friends, but Emma always helps him out when he is in trouble. Harry was well aware of the rumors, and he began belittling Emma's reputation and speaking disrespectfully of her to his friends behind her back. As a result of what

Harry said to them, all of Harry's pals began to despise Emma.

Harry used to hang out with Emma and her friends when he wanted to go. He tried to hide it when they went out with friends since he didn't want anybody to know, but even though he liked their company, but nothing changed; he still talked bitterly about her behind her back, despite the fact that she had helped him lots of times.

She has always enjoyed aiding others; she helped Harry in completing his projects, and she completed some of his tasks when he was unavailable, and she was the one who drew diagrams for his lab manual, which aided him. Harry, on the other hand, never acknowledged her efforts or the fact that she aided him on several occasions, even when she was in difficulty.

The most significant fact is that, despite being best friends, Emma, Peter, and Steve have animosity for one other, and Emma was the exception; they always felt envious when she was chatting to any other boy or even among themselves; if she spoke with Steve, Peter became jealous, and vice versa.

They, on the other hand, always try to keep their jealousy hidden.

So, let's learn a little more about Steve and Peter.

Peter is a man who exaggerates for everything and enjoys flirting with others, which he does frequently with Emma. He likes to be superior to others and aspires to be a leader, and he believes that he is flawless and handsome.

Steve, on the other hand, was a dunderhead who didn't know when to quit and was constantly irritating Emma for no apparent reason. He lacks the guts to begin a fight with her, but he still manages to annoy her and, without knowing it, he puts Emma in difficult situations.

She was a feminist who would argue with guys who belittled women, even if it was for fun. Peter had a habit of criticizing women, which irritated her, and they used to fight over it. And no one could stop her at that point since it was something she couldn't stand by and witness.

Steve has a friend Jack who has darkness at core of his heart and loves to inflict pain on others and he is Psycho among his friends sometimes he can be intimidating with a lot of anger. But all are fooled by his looks because he looks dumb.

Because she performed better in mathematics and Jack is good at another subject that Emma and Steve lacked. So, the three of them used to stay in college beyond class hours to study, and he used to mock Emma implicitly because he didn't know her well enough, so they both used Steve to communicate their ideas.

When they were in college, they would spend their time discussing their studies, and when they were bored, they would just do their own thing, such as listen to music or watch Netflix. Well, Jack had a habit of speaking harshly to Emma without even thinking about it, and as the examinations approached, things became more jumbled, and a few more were added due to test preparation, and they all used to spend the majority of their time conversing and less time studying.

Mark and Jason, who were pals with Harry, were among the newcomers. Mark and Jason were great friends, and they despise Harry, but he doesn't realize it.

They are all aware of the rumors that have been spread about her, and they all believe them. They have also spoken poorly about her in her absence.

When Emma told Steve and Jack that she wanted to go out to lunch with them right after they finished their examinations, Steve was happy with it, but Jack didn't want to be involved in such things and refused to join them and the plan turned into ashes.

Fortunately, Emma performed well in her examinations, and she was thrilled with her results because she did well in them and they are above her expectations, so she was completely surprised.

CHAPTER THREE

After completion of the exams Emma just watched Netflix in the semester break of one week later she should enroll for another semester and finally the day has come and it was a complete mess because she didn't have hard copy of her fee receipts and she missed her time slot so she undergone the enrollment process the very next day and unfortunately she doesn't have any friends in her new class except Molly who was her friend since she joined in college their houses were nearby so they were in same bus and they started talking to each other and they used to have a great talks in bus and in college they weren't that well acquainted.

By the second semester, Emma's patience had run out with Steve, and she began to scream at him, which wasn't necessarily a terrible thing because they had both grown accustomed to it, and there isn't a single day that goes by without Steve being disciplined by Emma but he never changes.

When her friends aren't there, Molly talks to Emma and never offers her to join them when she's alone, but Emma never does that with Molly; she regularly talks to her and welcomes her to join her when she's alone.

Molly and Emma used to go out after college on occasionally, and Emma never failed to accompany her whenever Molly asked, and they used to do whatever the hell they wanted while they were out, which is one of Emma's best memories because she enjoyed her company despite the fact that she never invited her to tag along when she was alone.

Emma once asked Steve for some help at a university fest, and he did it; however, Molly afterwards told Emma that she was only using Steve for her own needs, which enraged Emma and hurt her. As we all know, words cut deeper, so this moment has stayed in Emma's mind ever since. After a while, she calmed down and returned to normal.

Emma went out to lunch with Harry and Jason, as well as some of her friends, and they had a good time. Harry asked Emma for help since he liked one of her friends, and Emma tried to help him out, and Steve was also involved, but it didn't pan out as Harry had hoped, and everyone was fine by it.

Steve had a crush on a girl who was a childhood pal of his, but he kept it hidden from Emma and Peter. They both loved each other, so he went to see her on Valentine's Day and surprised her with chocolates, and they watched a movie together. Unfortunately, her father found out about it and called Steve, telling him not to mess with her daughter, and that if she ever tries to contact her again, he will deal with him harshly, and even told Steve's mother, which was heartbreaking. He told Emma and Peter everything at that time, and they both helped him get out of his despair and most of the credit goes to Emma.

Emma began to reply back to Mark in snapchat and the two began to converse. After a few days, another fest especially for girls was held on women's day, and Emma dressed up in a modern outfit and posted one of her favorites in snapchat, which was replayed and recorded by him, but when she asked him about it, he lied to her face and said he didn't record anything at all. They grew closer throughout the fest because they talked on the phone for hours until her phone's battery died.

At the time, Jack and Mark were friends because they were in the same class, and the three of them began to stay at the college after their classes for few hours to study and it was continued for tow to three days. At the time, a virus was spreading, and as a result, universities and all academics were handled online. Lockdown was imposed in every corner of the world at the time, and in that time three of them formed a group and began having conference calls, during which they studied and, when bored, talked about their personal lives.

Because of the virus epidemic, the semester's tests were held online, and they all assisted each other. Emma assisted Harry and Jason despite their insulting comments about her, but still she carried no grudges towards them. Emma was the only one who could forgive others for their mistakes, no matter how serious they were.

Mark began to like Emma because of her attitude and character, while Emma had a soft spot for Mark because he was raised by his uncle and he had no parents.

Emma, Mark, and Jack had a nice time together, and Mark was friends with Emma, calling her whenever he was free and chatting with her, and the same goes for Jack, but not as much as Mark.

Jack stopped calling Emma after a few days, and Mark has become their primary means of communication. As time passed, the distance between them grew. They all used to have daily online meetings. They used to join classes together, and it was fun for them. They got to know one other better, and their relationship grew stronger.

As usual, Jack and Emma continued the online meeting, and Jack was confused about why Mark had not shown up. As a result, he asked about it with Emma, who said that she had no clue. Jack and Emma continued their conversation and began calling him, but he did not return their calls. Jack was losing patience and becoming upset because Mark was not answering his calls. Emma asked that Jack to go to Mark's house to find out why he wasn't answering his phone, and Jack was fine by it, so they began looking for Mark's address.

After a while, Mark contacted Jack and informed him that his uncle had died that morning, and that he was very upset about it and he cried all day long, after that he had added Emma to the call and explained the situation.

Jack and Emma had a plan to help him get out of his depression, but since Jack wasn't very good at such things, it was up to Emma to handle it, and she was the only one who could do it. Later, Jason called Mark and got to know about the incident, and he cried for a while about it. Around the same time, there was a group project, and Mark, Emma, and Jack wanted to be a part of it, but Jason didn't like the idea, so he called Mark and asked him to join his team, and he said he'd talk to Jack and Emma about it. So, Jason called Jack and Emma and requested them to replace Mark from their team in exchange for one of his friends, Ron. They refused, and the situation escalated for while but Emma refused to give up on him. It was all thank to Emma she took stand at that moment and refused to give him.

Jason was frustrated, so he called Mark, and despite his grief, Jason began to bicker about the Team formation, insulting both Jack and Emma in the process. He also blamed Mark for being influenced by Emma, and he spoke extremely negatively about her. Mark couldn't respond to anything, so he recorded the entire call and shared it with the group. So that Jack and Emma could listen to it, and they did, and Emma was horrified to hear it, and she began crying, and she was severely hurt because of that call.

Later that day, Jack became furious with himself for remaining silent about the Jason call incident. So he contacted Ron and Jason and spoke and debated for a while about it. Jason apologized to Mark and also to Emma for insulting her. Emma forgave him, but she was still wounded because a simple apology doesn't make things better, especially after what he had done.

After a few days, they received notice that they needed to choose their expertise, and they all agreed to pick the same specialization, leaving Harry and Steve out. Emma decided to pick the specialization for Harry after he gave his credentials and begged her to do it if he didn't wake up the next morning. The next day, Harry failed to wake up, and Emma was confused about what to choose as his specialization, so she waited. After a while, there were only a few options available, so Harry was selected a specialization that was not the same as Mark's, Emma's, or anyone else's. As a result of his anger, he insulted Emma, and Steve was irritated about it as he got to know what happened. As a result, Steve called Harry and the two got into an argument.

CHAPTER FOUR

Things took some time to settle after that argument, and Harry dropped out of the group at that point, busy with his own affairs, and he never tried to contact anyone again.

Jack noticed Emma and Mark were both hiding something at first, but he thought they would eventually tell him what was going on, so he waited. Meanwhile, he began analyzing everything to get a clear picture of what was going on, and he came to the conclusion that he was the problem between them and that he was just a mess among them. As a result, he began to keep some distance, which Emma observed. Jack began responding sharply to Emma, and she was unable to talk to him about anything other than their academics. Jack started listening to music in his spare time while taking no action in meetings, avoiding both of them and acted independently. Meanwhile they were having fun spending time with each other.

Emma got addicted to Mark, and she loved and cared for him so much that she was willing to give up everything for him. They planned about their future together all of the time, and they decided that they should be together forever.

They used to quarrel over minor issues, but they got along fine again. However, Emma went to her relatives' house unexpectedly one day, and when she was talking to Mark about how she wasn't at home, the bell in their relatives' house rang. Emma's bell sound and her relatives' bell sound are, unfortunately, same. Mark, on the other hand, was not interested in her explanation instead raged at her, accusing her of lying to him and started dissing her which wounded her deeply. So she stopped talking to him and they maintained their daily routine with Jack as usual, despite their strained relationship.

Mark called Jack one day to explain the problem, stating they had gotten into a quarrel and she wouldn't talk to him. After that, Jack asked about the fight and requested that Emma to get along with him. Later, he became frustrated and simply left the problem in their hands, which they resolved themselves.

Emma wanted to tell Mark a happy birthday on his birthday, but she was lost in thought and didn't realise it was 12:00 a.m. Jack contacted Mark and noticed that he wasn't feeling well, so he called Emma to find out why. Emma then called Mark and expressed her birthday wishes to him and tried to find out why he was so depressed. At that moment they had a fight at the moment, and they decided not to speak to each other again.

Out of rage, Mark called Jack and explained that it wasn't his fault, that they had been in love for a long time, and that Emma was the one who started the quarrel. It all happened at midnight, and Jack helped Mark relax by assuring him that he would try to talk to her and told him to go to bed without making any more fuss about it.

Emma was depressed, and she fell asleep later. When Jack contacted her the next morning to find out what had happened, she told him she didn't feel comfortable around him, and she shared all of the problems she had faced in the previous months.

She told Jack that she doesn't get to have a free choice of will and that she should always do what he asks. He was the only one to make decisions, and he should have complete control over everything that happens in her life and the fact that he did not respect her privacy. She was enraged and frustrated because she has no say in what happens, and he also started a mess when they were just talking about their future plans and she said she would get a job, to which he objected and didn't encourage her. Later, she tried to educate him about the importance of employment, to which he agreed but still applied some stupid rules.

Mark insists on having his way, and he has never respected her judgments and forced her to do things his way against her will.

Jack was shocked to learn all of this because he had previously held a positive image of Mark, but that changed abruptly when he realised everything that happened he needed to stay by her side and assist her because she wasn't even capable of fighting for herself.

From that day Jack kept his distance from Mark because there is still much to know about him. So, Jack didn't want to get mixed up with him. Jack started supporting Emma and tried to help her out.

They wish to work on a project that will be due next semester. Mark and Emma first agreed to terms and decided to be friends, but that wasn't good enough; he messed it up again by asking Emma to be in a relationship with him, which enraged her, so she ended their friendship and joined another group for the project by that time the registrations were over, so they stayed in the same sections otherwise they would have been in different sections.

Emma was depressed because Mark kept calling her and asking to speak with him again, and if he was angry, he began yelling at her, which hurt her so terribly that she was on edge for several days. He stopped calling her after a few days, and he started asking Jack about Emma, and he asked him to try talking to her again, and he gave him some suggestions. Jack, on the other hand, refused to do them and instead told Mark about her opinions and feelings. He attempted to educate him about the faults he had made, but Jack failed miserably.

After a few days, Emma felt bad about scolding him and realised she had made a mistake, so she called Mark and told him she would only talk to him as friends. Mark was overjoyed to get the call, so he agreed to become buddies.

Jack was upset when he discovered what had happened because he had not been informed prior to the call being made to him. He calmed down after Emma when stated her reasons, which were that she didn't want to live with any guilt and that she wanted to get rid of it as soon as possible. She also stated that she was still angry by events in her relationship and that while she was comfortable with her relationship ending, she felt bad about the way in which it ended.

Since that day, they've been talking like friends whenever they have free time, and Emma has told them not to bring up the relationship again. He said that he was unconcerned about it. He just want to talk to her as friends and he was fine by it.

Emma wants everything to go smoothly, and she doesn't want any problems in their Trio group.

CHAPTER FIVE

It was the start of a new semester, and everyone was excited to return to college after the lockdown. Everyone is looking forward to meeting each other.

Mark was looking forward to meeting Emma, while Jack was adamant about staying in lockdown because he didn't want to meet anyone. Mark and Jack initially met on the first day of university, when they both went to class and later caught up with Emma. Mark wanted to speak with her, but she didn't respond well, and the day became a wreck once more.

Things took some time to settle down, and the days passed, and Jack used to go to classes without missing any, but Mark used to skip classes and spend the time with Emma most of the time, and they used to chat about the old stuff that had happened, and sometimes they argued about it over and over again.

After a few days, they decided to restart their relationship, and it was restarted. Jack was aware of this and kept his distance from both of them. Mark wanted to tell Jack about their connection, but Emma was angry because Jack was already acting strangely, so she needed some time to settle things, but Mark didn't listen to her and exposed their relationship. Jack had expected it, but as soon as he heard it, he was lost in his own thoughts and he was kind of shocked to hear it..

Emma was upset because Mark didn't listen to her, so she walked out. Mark went along with her to bring her back, but it was a total failure, so he requested Jack to get her into the room. Jack got her to come into class, and she left after a few minutes. Jack and Mark remained at college because they had some work to do.

The days pass, and Molly and Jason learn about their relationship because Mark and Emma used to spend time together. Jack gradually drifted apart from them because he dislikes having a large group of people in one area and always refuses to stay with them for a long period of time.

After few days it was on Emma's birthday Jason, Mark and Emma went out and had good time they spent that day with lots of happiness and after few days all of them went again for her birthday party including Molly, Steve, Peter, Jack and few others. Everyone is happy and all are enjoying their time together despite the small differences they had in between them.

During the college fests Emma and Molly decided to go to Marks place and it was their first time at his place they went out along with Jason and they had fun together. They had a fantastic time together that day, and they all went places and had a good time. On that evening, Jason and Mark decided to accompany Molly and Emma until they arrived at their places, and then they returned home. Mark and Emma were riding one bike, while Molly and Jason were on another. Since that day Molly and Jason also got closer to each other and they became good friends.

Molly and Jason remained in touch and they used to chat with each other and they both care for each other.

After a few days, it was Jason's birthday, and Emma and Molly decided to go to Jason's house with Mark, where they bought him cake and celebrated his birthday. On the same day, Emma wanted to surprise Jack, so she and Mark went to Jack's house, where he behaved cruelly, causing Emma to cry. Despite seeing Emma's tears, he acted like a monster and didn't even apologize. After that Mark and Emma joined with Molly and Jason and went out together and had a fantastic time before returning to their houses. Actually, Molly and Emma did not reveal what they were up to; they kept it a secret.

Jack took some time off and later called Emma to apologize for his misbehavior, and they both began to talk to each other normally, while Mark and Emma were in a relationship that no one knew about but the three of them do.

Everything was well until they started arguing again because he feels Emma has changed and she is no longer the same person she was before their breakup, and he believes it is due of what happened after their breakup. So Mark asked Jack about what happened in the month following their breakup. Jack went over everything, and Mark asked Emma the same question. Jack and Emma talked about it, and Jack was enraged but remained calm and Emma was upset about it.

Their disagreements grew worse by the day, and Emma tried her best to mediate them, but they quickly spiraled out of control.

It was time for their semester examinations, and on the first day of the exam, they had a disagreement and weren't talking to each other. So Emma studied with Steve, and Mark and Jack studied together for the exam. The next day in college, Mark went to see Emma, and Steve was sitting next her. Mark began yelling with them and shouting, but Steve remained silent since if anything went wrong, everyone would blame Emma.

On the same day, in the middle of his exam Mark walked out of the Exam hall and called his aunt and gave her the phone numbers of Jack and Emma, stating that he wasn't feeling well and that the charge in his phone was low.

After the examination, Jason informed Jack and Emma that Mark wasn't feeling well and wasn't returning his phone calls. Three of them began searching for him, but no one knows where he is. Mark's aunt and grandfather began phoning Emma, asking about Mark, but no one knew about it, and they became worried. Jack and Emma kept calling his phone, but he didn't answer.

After an hour, he called back and said he wasn't feeling well, so he slept in the campus dispensary room, where he awoke soon afterward. Jack knows it was a lie because he sent one of his friends to check in the dispensary rooms, but he remained calm after that Mark phoned Jack again after a few minutes and told him that he called one of his friends who was close to college and he went outside and went for a checkup. He conveyed the same to his aunt and grandad and to Emma.

Mark got into another argument with Emma, claiming that she was the reason he wasn't feeling well, that he didn't do well in his exam, and that he put everything on her. After that, he became agitated and yelled at Emma, who taped everything and forwarded it to Jack. When Mark found out that she had sent those call recordings to Jack, he was angry, and he added both of them to the call and made a big deal about it.

Emma was very depressed, and his words greatly wounded her. Mark became enraged and yelled at both Jack and Emma for the next two days, focusing primarily on Emma. So Jack stopped talking to Mark, and Emma followed same. Jack tried to reason with Mark, but it did not go as planned, and they parted ways.

CHAPTER SIX

Everyone believed it was over when they parted ways, but it was just the beginning of the commotion and ruckus that was to come.

Molly came to visit Emma one day and they both talked to each other and Emma conveyed what had happened between her and Mark and later that night Molly called Emma again and told her that Mark isn't at his home and Molly requested Emma to talk to him and settle this then Emma called Mark and insisted him to go home but he refused for a while he said that he would agree to it but in return he wanted her to talk to him as there are no other options ahead Emma agreed to it Then Emma was enraged with Molly because she knew he wasn't at home when she met her, but she kept it a secret.

The next day, Mark contacted Emma to chat, and she warned him not to blackmail her again, and she wasn't interested in talking to him, so Mark became enraged and insulted her, causing a commotion.

After they split up, Mark began to post their photos together online, and by seeing them, everyone knew that Mark and Emma were in love, and it spread throughout the entire college. It was a frustrating moment for Emma because she never expected him to make everything public when things weren't going well between them.

Emma began to worry about the things she would have to face in the near future since everyone began to question her and she was in a complete state of confusion. When things were like this, Mark began phoning Emma again, blackmailing her that he would make a greater mess than before, and threatening her that he would expose their connection to her parents, which scared Emma. She had not expected such threats from Mark, so she was depressed and unsure what to do. She made a decision and gathered the strength to tell her parents what had happened. But she was too terrified to do anything, and she became buried in her own thoughts. She told everything to her parents moments later, and they supported her and made her feel comfortable, which surprised her because she didn't predict them to be that supportive.

A few days later, Emma received a call from an unknown number, and it was one of Mark's friends who claimed to be his cousin, and he inquired about all that had occurred and wanted to resolve their differences. Emma told Mark's cousin about how much she had suffered, which surprised him because he never expected him to be like that. After the call, he conveyed everything to Mark, and as a result, Mark called Emma again and yelled at her for telling him everything, and he blamed her for not showing any respect while talking to his cousin, who was one year senior to us.

Except for Jack, no one knows Emma informed her parents everything that had happened, and he never talked about it with anyone, so no one truly knows. As things were, one day Mark contacted Emma's father and said he needed to speak to him, but because her father was in the office, he said he would call later. Emma's father called Mark the next day to speak with him about the previous day. Then Mark told his father about their relationship and asked her father to talk to Emma about it. He also said that he would send photos of them together to her father, but her father refused to see the photos and simply replied that he doesn't want to see any photos and that he trusts her daughter and believes what she has told him. Emma was blessed because her father backed her, but she was also unhappy because she thought she had betrayed them, and she had not anticipated Mark to do that to her.

Emma's father advised Mark not to tamper with Emma again, and he also stated that if they want to be friends, he has no objections and is fine with it, but anything more than that would be bad. Mark lost his words and remained silent, unsure of what to do, and the call was ended.

Throughout the entire conversation between Mark and Emma's Father, Mark was very rude and it was a rather frustrating thing, and while Emma was beside her father along with her Mother, everyone listened to their conversation and after the whole conversation came to an end, they advised Emma to stay away from him and her Father asked her to inform him if anything went wrong, which she gladly agreed to.

This was a heartwarming event for Emma since she was receiving more love and support from her parents, which she was pleased about, and her parents began spending more time with her from that day forward, which she was overjoyed about.

One day, Jack received a call from Mark's cousin, who asked him if he had told Emma's father that Mark was torturing her, and Jack said that he hadn't, but Mark blamed Jack anyway, and it became a mess for quite some time, and Jack came to know that Mark's cousin had also called Steve, and he was tortured by them, and Steve didn't tell anyone because he has no idea what is going on.

Right after that, Jack called Steve and asked him about everything that had happened, then Jack got a clear picture of what was going on around him and conveyed the same to Emma, and they decided to stay put until there was more trouble, and if anything went wrong, Jack and Steve decided to fight head on without delay. Meanwhile, Emma received another call from his cousin, and they discussed everything, and everything was resolved for the time being.

From that day forward, he tried to mess with her every once in a while and continued until the semester break was over and it was a new semester and they got into different sections but it wasn't over there was still a lot more to come as he was still fixated on her and Emma has a soft corner in her heart for him no matter what he has done.

CHAPTER SEVEN

As it was the start of a new semester and everyone was pleased to be back at college, there were some who wished they had longer holidays, but everything must come to an end.

The semester started, and everyone knew about Mark and Emma's relationship, and some of them got a hint that they weren't on good terms, and some tried to solve it, while others tried to take advantage of it. The biggest surprise of the semester was Molly, Sofia, and Mark becoming good friends, which surprised almost everyone because no one imagined such a tragic mix as a new beginning.

Nobody knows why they had to get together. Molly had turned on Emma, and she was now a Mark puppet. Initially, Emma, Jack, Steve, and Peter used to hang out in college, but as their timetables clashed, Steve and Peter left, and Jack used to be around Emma. But one fine day when Jack wasn't around, Mark tried to talk to Emma, and she tried her best to avoid it, but because she has a soft spot in her heart for him, she responded and they are friends again, and she joined with Molly and Sofia that day, and when she returned home, she told Jack about it, and he didn't take it well at first but he tried to understand the situations moments later.

Now, Mark tried to get back together with Emma as lovers, but she was not up to it, so he only talked to her and brought up old issues and questioned her about them, and he never understood his faults, still he blamed her for everything. Emma tried to argue back, but it wasn't enough because there were more people supporting Mark at the moment, and no one cared to hear her side of the tale.

These debates lasted for days, and Mark would listen to anything Molly and Sofia had to say and then ask Emma about it, starting a conflict and arguing about it until he eventually blamed her, deciding that he had never made such mistakes and that each and every mistake was created only by Emma.

Emma lost control and then erupted in a fight again, this time involving Emma's brother and Emma's father, because when Emma and Mark were arguing about all of these incidents, Emma's brother overheard it and took the phone from Emma and tried to talk to Mark, but Mark was very rude and didn't show any sign of respect to them, which was a big mistake he made because now he has lost each and every option that could make him dream come true.

Emma's brother called Peter and tried to find out what had happened, but Peter threw gasoline to the fire by adding his own fantasies and creating a fairytale with himself as its major protagonist, which he conveyed to Steve later and begged him to keep the same story going.

Emma and Jack found out about it when Steve told them, and Emma burst into tears because she was frightened her brother would come to college to complain about it, making the situation even worse than it is, and she has no idea who to trust and who not to trust.

She tried talking to her father in the hopes of getting an answer and everything was fine and they left matters in

Emma's hands to deal with and they would step in if she couldn't handle it she is glad that they gave her a chance again and she doesn't want to misuse it so she conveyed everything she wants to say to Mark the topic came to a temporary halt.

Emma made a new friend, Alice, in her class, and they grew close quickly. They enjoyed each other's company, and she was delighted to be around her. She and Alice are two peas in a pod, and Alice was a precious person that Emma met in college.

They both enjoyed each other's company and shared their stories, and they used to aid each other when they were in trouble. A few days later, Mark began to talk with Emma again, and this time it was a little different; he said that he doesn't want to be with Molly and Sofia because they can't be trusted, and he asked Emma to help him with his academics; Emma lost her words and agreed to help him with his academics, which was rather frustrating for Jack, but it happened anyway. Emma used to spend her leisure time with Mark and Alice from then on since if she was alone, he would make things worse by talking about the past topics, so to avoid that she asked Alice to help her and she was happy to help her out.

Mark used to take Emma's help and told her that he wasn't talking with Molly or Sofia, but he was with them when Emma wasn't there, and Emma didn't know about it until Jack told her. Jack confirmed that fact with his friend Alex, who had adored Sofia and then became a mess once Mark began talking to her, and he was sad and enraged with him.

Jack introduced Alex to Emma, and they instantly became friends. Mark didn't like that, and he began to fight with her. The fight ended fast because it was his mistake, but he later pinned it on her.

After having conversations together Alex got the wind of what was happening and he was glad that he wasn't around Sofia anymore, Jack and Emma also came to know many things from Alex and they were glad to meet each other and they became a group real fast and they used to spend time with each other and everyone are happy about it and as the current semester came to an end they decide to be together in the next semester.

When Mark saw Alex take a picture with Emma and post it, he became enraged and made a commotion by telling everyone and gathering people for a showdown the next day when Mark saw Alex he came towards him and tried to boss around but it was all in vain when Emma came and took Alex from that place which made it clear that she has no problem taking a picture with him and no one should be bothered about it everyone who came to support Mark lost their words and went quietly. He still wanted to fight on that day afternoon, but no one heard from him, and when Alex asked one of his friends who tried to support him, he claimed that Mark just compromised about it.

From that day forward, it was truly a fresh beginning for Emma, as she was relieved that Alex would fight for her, and that day, many of her friends were willing to provide a help, which she was delighted by, and her pleasure was at an all-time high.

Despite the difficulties, she made many friends who supported her through it all, and Emily is one of them. She may not constantly be beside her, but if Emma was in need, she did her best to support her.

CHAPTER EIGHT

Emma's narrative hasn't ended, and it won't in the near future because she has a long way to go and the path isn't always full of flowers; it's the path of thrones. She relies on her friends and family for support, and she's always grateful to have them in her life.

Mark put her through a lot, but so did Jack, Steve, Peter, Molly, Sofia, Harry, and Jason, all of them had their own agendas and tried to rub it on Emma despite the odds. Mark pushed her into a relationship she wasn't ready for. Jack pushed her to act in accordance with his plans, and he wounded her even more as a result of his rage, which was no excuse because he was also the reason of her pain and suffering. Steve and Peter alternated playing with her, lying to her and doing things behind her back that no one knew about. Harry only used Emma for academic purposes, and he used to gossip behind her back. Emma was deceived by Jason and Molly at a time when she needed them the most they played with her faith. Sofia always made matters worse by talking behind people's backs, which caused a lot of controversy..

There are many things that upset Emma, and no one cared about how much pressure they were putting on her to do everything flawlessly without making any mistakes, but everyone is forgetting a simple fact: she isn't a goddamn machine; she is a human, and humans are bound to make mistakes and that is what makes us human.

She always tried her best to help people around her and she was innocent and kindhearted no matter what the circumstances were. It is true that she met many people in her life and most of them caused her pain and suffering but she tried her best not to hurt them because she understands the pain and she does not want to be like them.

Everyone tells Emma what she should do with her life, leaving no room for her to think about herself, but they expect her to worry about everyone else. No one ever asked her what she really wanted; she was forced to do everything. She hadn't experienced true freedom and happiness in her life; she wanted to enjoy everything she could obtain, but it wasn't possible with so many monsters around.

Emma trusts people easily and that is a good thing but there are two sides to a coin in the same way there will be damage caused for putting trust in wrong people and she can't differentiate between both of them.

Emma trusts people readily, which is a wonderful thing, but there will be consequences for putting her confidence in the wrong people, and she can't tell the difference between them it is rather disappointing about her.

It's okay to be hurt and feel pain, but we should try to overcome it one day or another because if we don't, that suffering will drag us to the pits of hell and no one can help us get out of the pain and suffering. We can get people to support us, but no one can bear the pain with us to make it easier, so we should take the first step to climb out of that pit.

Emma lost hope in her life and just wanted to die since she realized she had trusted the wrong guy when Mark turned on her. She couldn't stand the anguish he caused her, and it was still affecting her, and it will continue to affect her as long as she finds happiness, but the amazing part is that she didn't give up and continued to battle for her self-esteem, and she will fight till she is happy.The tale itself is based on true events; it may not be appealing or have plots and twists like movies or fairytales; however, let us return to reality and imagine Emma's suffering and how difficult it is when you are all alone and everyone you once trusted has turned against you, and the love of your life tries to control you according to his wishes, and everyone is projecting their thoughts and dreams onto you when you are not ready for it.

Conclusion

In conclusion, even though everyone expected things to settle, they didn't, and everything is leading to greater chaos. We can only hope that nothing worse happens and she finds happiness and freedom.

Thank you for your time

www.ingramcontent.com/pod-product-compliance
Lightning Source LLC
Chambersburg PA
CBHW031003180726
47993CB00018B/1548